Sunshine

SUNSHINE.

Jesse Bennett

Archway Publishing books may be ordered through booksellers or by contacting:

Archway Publishing
1663 Liberty Drive
Bloomington, IN 47403
www.archwaypublishing.com
1 (888) 242-5904

ISBN: 978-1-4808-7797-9 (sc)
ISBN: 978-1-4808-7798-6 (hc)
ISBN: 978-1-4808-7796-2 (e)

Printed in China.

Archway Publishing rev. date: 5/23/2019

ARCHWAY
PUBLISHING

Sunshine

This book is dedicated to the sunshines in my
life, my sweet Madison Eve and Samuel Everett…
my Eve and Evi! Thank you to my husband
Ryan for all of his support & encouragement;
thank you for making our home a yoga house!

To all the families encouraging kindness
and goodness in their children, thank you
for making the world a brighter place! From
my yoga house to yours, I honor you!

Contents

"Wake up sleepy heads, blink your eyes open let's pop out of bed! An exciting day, fresh and new is awake and waiting for you!" Mama Owl said happily!

OUR NEST

"Waiting for us?" Eve and Evi say with twinkling eyes and happy feet!

"Yes, a brand-new day for you to meet! What will make today amazing, fantastic, outstanding and fun? YOU my loves, so shine like the sun," said their mama with a tilt of her head and a nod of her beak.

"You are a lighthouse. A shimmering star!"

"Lead with your heart and love who you are!"

"From the tips of your wings, to the sparkle in your eyes!
You light up this world with your sunshine!"

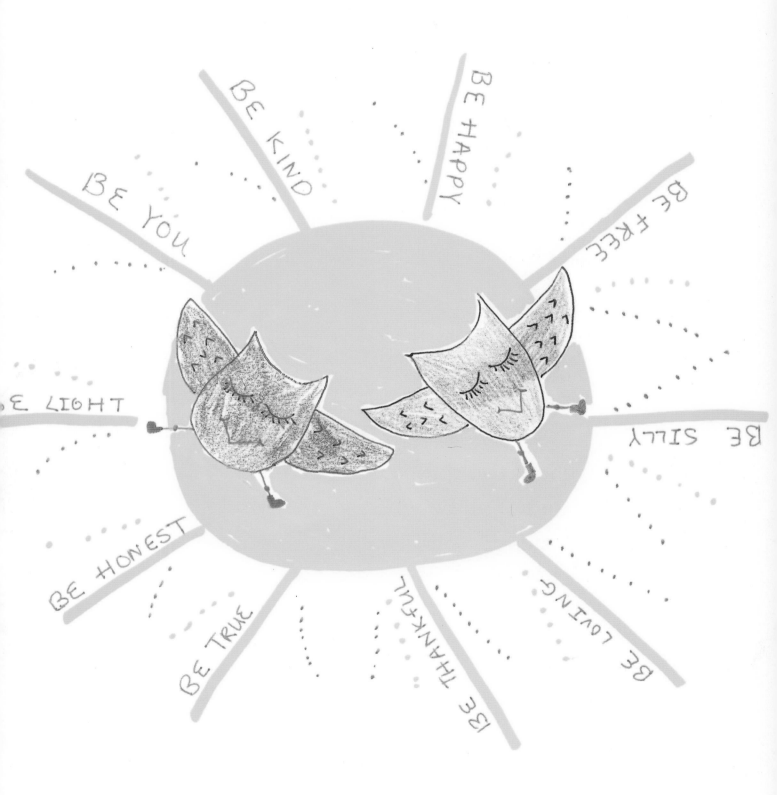

"Be the good, the happy,
be free! Most of all be who
you are meant to be."

6

"What if a rain cloud pours down on just me? What if I fall playing ball and scrape up my right knee? What if my lunch pail jumps out of my bag, and my left sock starts to sag?"

"Some days are off, funky out of whack. Breathe deep and know tomorrow you will be on track. Lift your heart, smile if you can. Remember these clouds will part and the sun will shine again. Let's practice together so when those cloudy days appear, we breathe through it together as a team and find your cheer." Mama said and gave Eve and Evi the biggest hug!

"You remember my loves to shine like the sun and choose happy thoughts and soon you will become a hip hop happy little bird spreading cheer here and there! It is your happy heart that will help those clouds clear."

"To make sure your day feels the best it can be…"
Mama chirped. "Always stick with friends who
feel like sunshine," chimed in Eve and Evi!

"Yes, and YOU be the sunshine too! It is your one of a kind light that makes you beautifully YOU! Today WILL be awesome, the BEST, out of sight! Remember YOU are the only one who can SHINE your light!"

Your light is so beautiful to Me!

"There is a light that shines out from your eyes. It makes the world smile and it is no surprise! It comes from your heart, your beautiful soul. Everyone has a light that's their very own. You shimmer and glimmer and twinkle like a star. Always remember how special you are!"

Sunshine I AM AFFIRMATION

I am a light
I am kind
I am strong
I am smart
I am proud to be me
I am a sunshine
I make this world a brighter place

Samuel — 6

Age 9

Sunshine Meditation

Breathe with me as the sky brightens and the day wakes
Breathe with me as the birds chirp and build their nests
Breathe with me as you sit up tall reaching
the crown of your head to the sky
Breathe with me as you lead with your heart
Shine so bright
Be kind
Be YOU
Stay true to what makes your heart happy
Speak kind words to yourself
Speak kind words to others
You are a shining star
I believe in you. You make the world a better more
beautiful place by being who you are. Breathe
with me sweet one and know you are loved
bigger than the sky and all the stars in it!

Feel Better Tool Kit

♥ 3 big hot air balloon breaths – turning your palms up and as you breathe in they rise and as you breath out turn your palms down and let your breath calm you

Hot Air Balloon Breath

palms up - let your balloon rise as you breathe in .....
palms down - let your balloon lower as you breathe out

Open up your Feel Better Tool Kit anytime you need a little cheer

♥ Kick your legs up the wall
♥ Get some fresh air
♥ Snuggle a family pet
♥ A big bear hug
♥ Draw a picture
♥ Share how your heart feels
♥ Play your favorite song

Journal Questions

3 things that make me smile are...

3 things that I am grateful for are...

How can I shine my brightest today?

Who needs my sunshine today?

I feel most like sunshine when...

What can I do to be a sunshine friend?